MONTVILLE TWP. PUBLIC LIBRARY
90 Horseneck Road
Montville, N.J. 07045

9-15-09

ER
Moncu
Moncure, Jane Belk.

Short "e" and long "e"
play a game /

W9-BXT-374

0 1021 0146306 9

02-22-04
ON LINE

Montville Twp. Public Library
90 Horseneck Road
Montville, N.J. 07045-9626

PLEASE DO NOT REMOVE CARDS
FROM POCKET
There will be a charge if
not returned with book.

# Short "e" and Long "e"
## Play a Game

# The Child's World®

Copyright © 2002 by The Child's World®, Inc.
All rights reserved. No part of this book may be
reproduced or utilized in any form or by any means
without written permission from the publisher.
Printed in the United States of America.

**Library of Congress Cataloging-in-Publication Data**
Moncure, Jane Belk.
Short "e" and long "e" play a game / by Jane Belk Moncure ; illustrated by Norman Young.
p. cm.
Summary: A brief story in which characters representing the short "e"
sound and the long "e" sound look for these vowels in different words.
ISBN 1-56766-929-8 (lib. bdg.)
[1. English language—Vowels—Fiction.]  I. Young, N. (Norman), ill. II. Title.
PZ7.M739 Sg 2001
[E]—dc21
00-010849

0 1021 0146306 9

# Short "e" and Long "e"
## Play a Game

Jane Belk Moncure

*illustrated by* Norman Young

This is  . She has a special sound.

Egg

begins with her short **e** sound.

So does elephant.

egg

elephant

This is  long e. He has a different sound.

Emu

begins with his long "e" sound.

So does eagle.

eagle

emu

Can you hear the short e

and the long e sounds?

One day, Short "e" said,
"Let's play a game. I will look
for my sound in words.

eagle

emu

You can look for your sound in words. We'll see who can find the most words."

Short e found an elk

and an Eskimo.

Then short e found an elf.

"I will win!" she said.

**Long e** found eels.

Then  found an egret.

egret

"No! I will win!" he said.

egg

elephant

elk

elf

Eskimo

Short e

counted. "I win," she said.
"I have the most words."

emu

egret

eagle

eels

Long e counted.

"No! No! No!" he said.

"I will use my eyes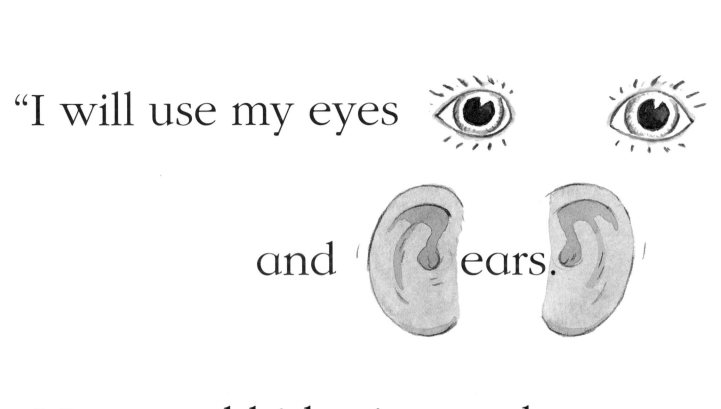

and ears.

My sound hides in words.
I will find words with my
sound in the middle of them."

found the sea

for the eels.

Long e found a

seal in the sea.

He also found a sheep.

Then he found trees

for the eagle

and emu

and egret.

"Now I will win!" said e.

"No! No! No!" said 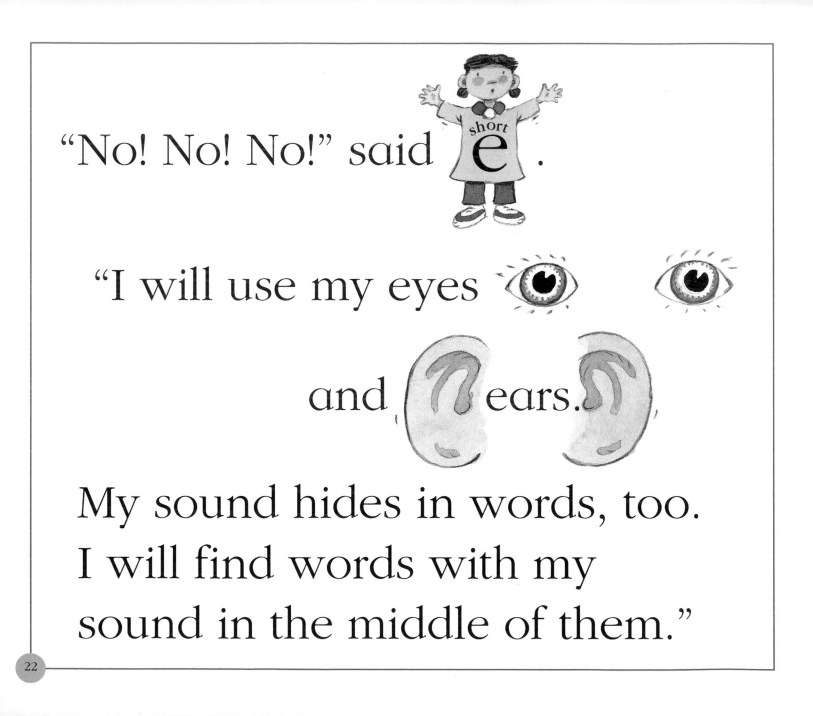 short e .

"I will use my eyes

and ears.

My sound hides in words, too.
I will find words with my
sound in the middle of them."

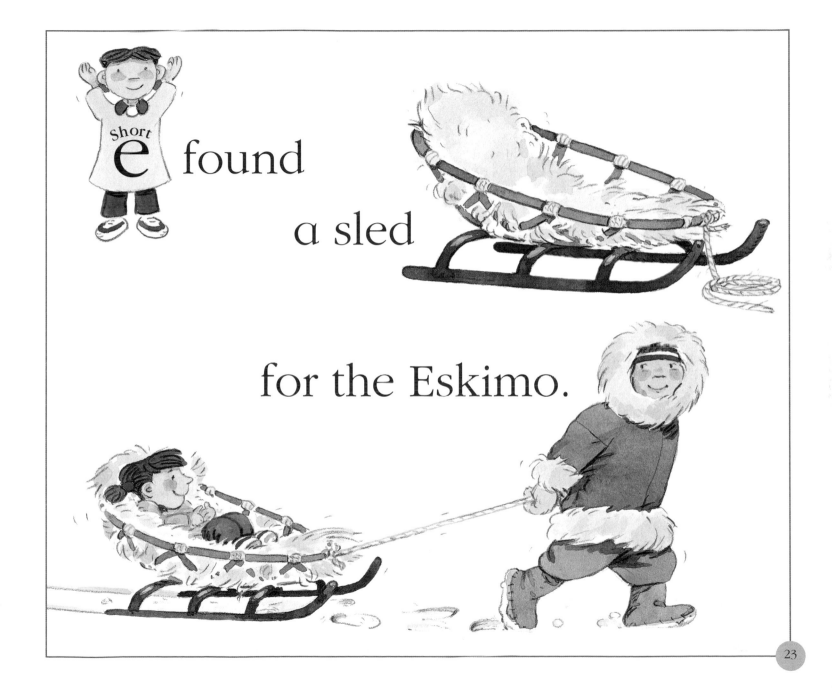

Short e found

a sled

for the Eskimo.

Then  found

a bed    for the elf.

Then she found a hen

and a nest for the egg.

"Now I win!" said short e.

elephant

hen

egg

nest

sled

elk

Eskimo

short e

bed

elf

Can you tell who won?

emu

egret

eagle

trees

sheep

seal

sea

eels

long e

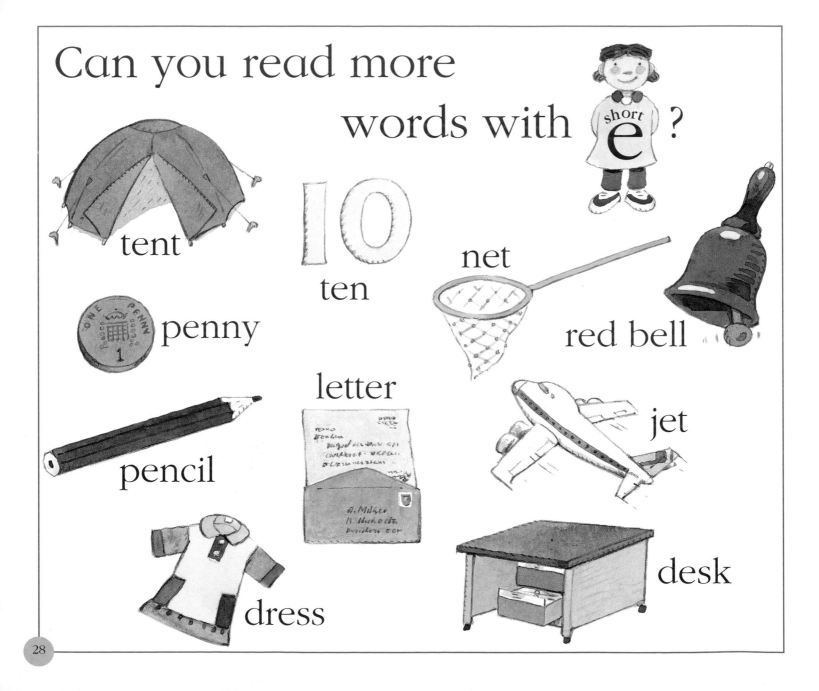

Can you read more words with short e ?

tent

ten

net

red bell

penny

letter

jet

pencil

dress

desk

28

Can you read more words with **long e**?

tea

queen

wheel

teeth

peach

beets

zebra

key

leaf

29

# Now you make up a game!

# ABOUT THE AUTHOR AND ILLUSTRATOR

**Jane Belk Moncure** began her writing career when she was in kindergarten. She has never stopped writing. Many of her children's stories and poems have been published, to the delight of young readers, including her son Jim, whose childhood experiences found their way into many of her books.

Mrs. Moncure's writing is based upon an active career in early childhood education. A recipient of an M.A. degree from Columbia University, Mrs. Moncure has taught and directed nursery, kindergarten, and primary grade programs in California, New York, Virginia, and North Carolina. As a former member of the faculties of Virginia Commonwealth University and the University of Richmond, she taught prospective teachers in early childhood education.

Mrs. Moncure has travelled extensively abroad, studying early childhood programs in the United Kingdom, The Netherlands, and Switzerland. She was the first president of the Virginia Association for Early Childhood Education and received its award for outstanding service to young children. A resident of North Carolina, Mrs. Moncure is currently a full-time writer and educational consultant. She is married to Dr. James A. Moncure, former vice president of Elon College.

**Norman Young** spent his childhood on a small farm nestled at the foot of the Preseli Hills in Pembrokeshire, South West Wales. He started his artistic career as a film animator in London and then in Zagreb. Eventually he settled in Devon, where he lives beside a river that runs between the moors and the sea. It was here that he started his work as an illustrator of children's books. Norman has always had a lifelong interest in history and travel. Taking a month off work each year, he visits new places either by train or by bicycle—and he never goes anywhere without his sketchbook.

MONTVILLE TWP. PUBLIC LIBRARY
90 Horseneck Road
Montville, N.J. 07045